Presented to
Tulsa City-County Library
by the
**Anne V. Zarrow Library Books for Children Fund**

*Tulsa Community Foundation*

# *Dear Parent:*
# *Your child's love of reading starts here!*

Every child learns to read in a different way and at his or her own speed. Some go back and forth between reading levels and read favorite books again and again. Others read through each level in order. You can help your young reader improve and become more confident by encouraging his or her own interests and abilities. From books your child reads with you to the first books he or she reads alone, there are I Can Read Books for every stage of reading:

### SHARED READING
Basic language, word repetition, and whimsical illustrations, ideal for sharing with your emergent reader

### BEGINNING READING
Short sentences, familiar words, and simple concepts for children eager to read on their own

### READING WITH HELP
Engaging stories, longer sentences, and language play for developing readers

### READING ALONE
Complex plots, challenging vocabulary, and high-interest topics for the independent reader

**I Can Read Books** have introduced children to the joy of reading since 1957. Featuring award-winning authors and illustrators and a fabulous cast of beloved characters, I Can Read Books set the standard for beginning readers.

A lifetime of discovery begins with the magical words **"I Can Read!"**

*Visit www.icanread.com for information*
*on enriching your child's reading experience.*

*Para mi sobrinita Teresa Clementina.
¡Te quiero!
—E.O.*

*To my neighbors who have become
dear friends along the years.
—A.L.*

I Can Read® and I Can Read Book® are trademarks of HarperCollins Publishers.

Reina Ramos: Neighborhood Helper
Text copyright © 2024 by Emma Otheguy
Illustrations copyright © 2024 by Andrés Landazábal
All rights reserved. Manufactured in Malaysia.
No part of this book may be used or reproduced in any manner whatsoever without written permission except in the case of brief quotations embodied in critical articles and reviews. For information address HarperCollins Children's Books, a division of HarperCollins Publishers,
195 Broadway, New York, NY 10007.
www.icanread.com

Library of Congress Control Number: 2023948435
ISBN 978-0-06-322325-7 (trade bdg.) — ISBN 978-0-06-322324-0 (pbk.)

Book design by Elaine Lopez
24 25 26 27 28   COS   10 9 8 7 6 5 4 3 2 1

# Reina Ramos
## Neighborhood Helper

by Emma Otheguy
pictures by Andrés Landazábal

HARPER
*An Imprint of HarperCollinsPublishers*

In the fall,

Abuela and I look for yellow.

Fall leaves, traffic lights,

and the big sign at school:

We are doing a food drive!

We are going to collect cans of food to give to a shelter. If our class collects the most, we will get a pizza party!

I want to start collecting cans

as soon as I get home.

But Abuela has other plans.

We're bringing food to Ms. Mia.

She lives downstairs

and has a new baby.

I help Abuela put black beans, rice, and meat into containers to take downstairs.

Ms. Mia welcomes us in.

"¡Gracias!" Ms. Mia says.

She's happy we brought food because she's too tired to cook.

Baby Pablito is so cute!

I tickle his soft feet.

"¡Tiki-tiki!" I say.

He smiles.

Then I help Ms. Mia change his diaper.
I'm not afraid of stinky!

When I get to school the next day, there's already a big pile of cans in the box outside Ms. Fox's door. Her class is way ahead of us!

I feel bad.

Abuela and I were tired
after helping with baby Pablito.
We forgot to collect cans!

At recess, Mr. Li's class has an emergency meeting. We won't let Ms. Fox's class get the pizza party!

Nora will paint a beautiful sign.

Carlos will ask his dad to hang it up.

Lila and her dog will go door to door.

No one can say no to Chico!

I think hard.

Everyone else has a plan.

I want to help my class,

and I want to win!

¿Cómo?

How can I get more cans?

At home, I tell Abuela.

We need to go get more cans.

"¿Por favor?" I beg.

But she's busy!

"I can't go to the store," she says.

"But you can take these."

Two cans! That's it?

There are more in the cabinet,

but Abuela says she needs those.

What is my class going to say?

Luckily, my friends got tons of cans.
When I look at the boxes,
I think we have almost as many cans
as Ms. Fox's class!

The principal counts the cans.

Ms. Fox's class has sixty-two.

Then she counts our cans.

I cross my fingers.

I know we will win!

"Fifty-eight, fifty-nine, sixty . . ."

"Sixty-one. Ms. Fox's class wins!"

We lost by only one can!

I choke back tears.

It's not fair!

It's all Abuela's fault!

She wouldn't give me more cans!

Ms. Fox's class gets the pizza party.

Mr. Li's class does worksheets.

I can smell the yummy pizza.

I HATE worksheets.

That afternoon,

I don't talk to Abuela.

And I giggle when baby Pablito

spits up on her.

"What's wrong, Reina?"

Ms. Mia asks.

I tell her.

"Reina!" Abuela says.

"It's not about winning!"

Ms. Mia puts her arm around me.

"I know how you feel.

But I have an idea.

I'm going to bring some things
to my church tonight.

Why don't you come with me?"

Ms. Mia packs up diapers.

Abuela adds a meal she made.

I help carry things.

We put down the boxes

and join the other families.

I like sharing food and diapers.

I make silly faces,

and baby Pablito gurgles.

He makes people so happy!

Abuela was right.

The food drive was about helping, not winning.

A pizza party would have been fun— but it's fun to be with our neighbors!

Mami is waiting for us at home.

Guess what?

We're having pizza for dinner!

I give Abuela a hug and I dig in!

# Glossary

**¿Cómo?**: How?

**¡Gracias!**: Thank you!

**Por favor**: Please

**¡Tiki-tiki!**: Tickle-tickle!